Peter Pan

Dorling Kindersley
LONDON, NEW YORK, SYDNEY, DELHI,
PARIS, MUNICH and JOHANNESBURG

Editor Rebecca Smith
Project Art Editor Lisa Lanzarini
Senior Editor Marie Greenwood
Senior Art Editor Jane Thomas
Managing Art Editor Jacquie Gulliver
US Editor Constance M. Robinson
Picture Research Mariana Sonnenberg
DTP Designer Kim Browne
Production Joanne Rooke

Published in the United States by DK Publishing, Inc.
375 Hudson Street, New York, New York 10014

First American Edition, 1998
Paperback edition published in 2000
8 10 9 7

J. M. Barrie donated his copyright to *Peter Pan* to Great Ormond Street Children's Hospital in 1929, and a royalty from the sale of this book will therefore be paid to the Hospital.

Published in Great Britain by Dorling Kindersley Limited.

A catalog record is available from the Library of Congress
ISBN: 0-7566-1275-6

Color reproduction by Bright Arts
Printed in China by L.Rex Printing Co., Ltd.

Acknowledgements
The publisher would like to thank the following for their kind permission to reproduce the photographs:
a=above; b=below; c=center; l=left; r=right; t=top

Catherine Ashmore: 47c; **Bridgeman Art Library:** Spink & Son Ltd., London, *Autumn in Kensington Gardens*, Wallace, James 7br; **J. Allan Cash Ltd:** 7br; **© Disney:** 47cr; **Mary Evans Picture Library:** 6tl, 8tr, 9bl, 25cl, 40br, **Hulton Getty:** 48tl; **Great Ormond St.:** 26cr, 48bl; **Mander & Mitchenson:** 46bl, 48c; **National Maritime Museum:** 38tl; **The Robert Opie Collection:** 11tl, 15bl; **Retna Pictures:** Michael Putcano 6cr; **Tony Stone Images:** 7bl; **Frederick Warne & Co:** The Forget-me-not Fairy from *Flower Fairies of the Summer* by Cicely Mary Barker Copyright © The Estate of Cicely Mary Barker, 1925, 1990, 37br.

Dorling Kindersley would particularly like to thank the following people: Kit Palmer, Raymond Lunnon, and Nicholas Baldwin at Great Ormond Street Hospital; Claire Jones for models; Gary Ombler for photography; Lisa Lanzarini for artwork borders.

DORLING KINDERSLEY *CLASSICS*

Peter Pan

By J. M. BARRIE

Adapted by Michael Johnstone

Illustrated by Chris Molan

A Dorling Kindersley Book

John
Wendy
Peter Pan
Michael
Tinker Bell
Mr. Darling
Mrs. Darling
Nana

The Indians
Starkey
Tiger Lily
Smee
Captain
Hook
The lost
boys
The crocodile

Contents

The Perfect Childhood

J. M. BARRIE CREATED Peter Pan at the beginning of the 20th century. This was a peaceful period in England, and in many ways the perfect time to be a child. People were more concerned about children's welfare, education, and happiness than ever before.

✷ A LONDON HOME
Barrie's story begins in the Darling's family home in Bloomsbury, central London. Like many parents, the Darlings provided a safe, comfortable environment for their children, full of toys and books – protected from the adult world outside.

Children often had their own floor at the top of the house with two connected rooms, a day-nursery to play in and a night-nursery to sleep in.

Teddy bears were popular toys.

Many children were allowed into their parents' rooms only on special occasions.

✷

The servants usually lived downstairs. Children hardly ever saw the servants' quarters.

A wealthy family at this time would have a maid, a nanny, and sometimes a cook. The Darlings cannot afford a nanny.

✷ KENSINGTON GARDENS

Barrie lived close to Kensington Gardens in London and often took his large dog, Porthos, for walks there. This is his map of the gardens, and many of the features remain to this day. In Barrie's map, the gardens become the home of fairies and runaway children – and most important of all, the first home of Peter Pan.

✷ PETER PAN

Today, Peter Pan's statue stands in Kensington Gardens.

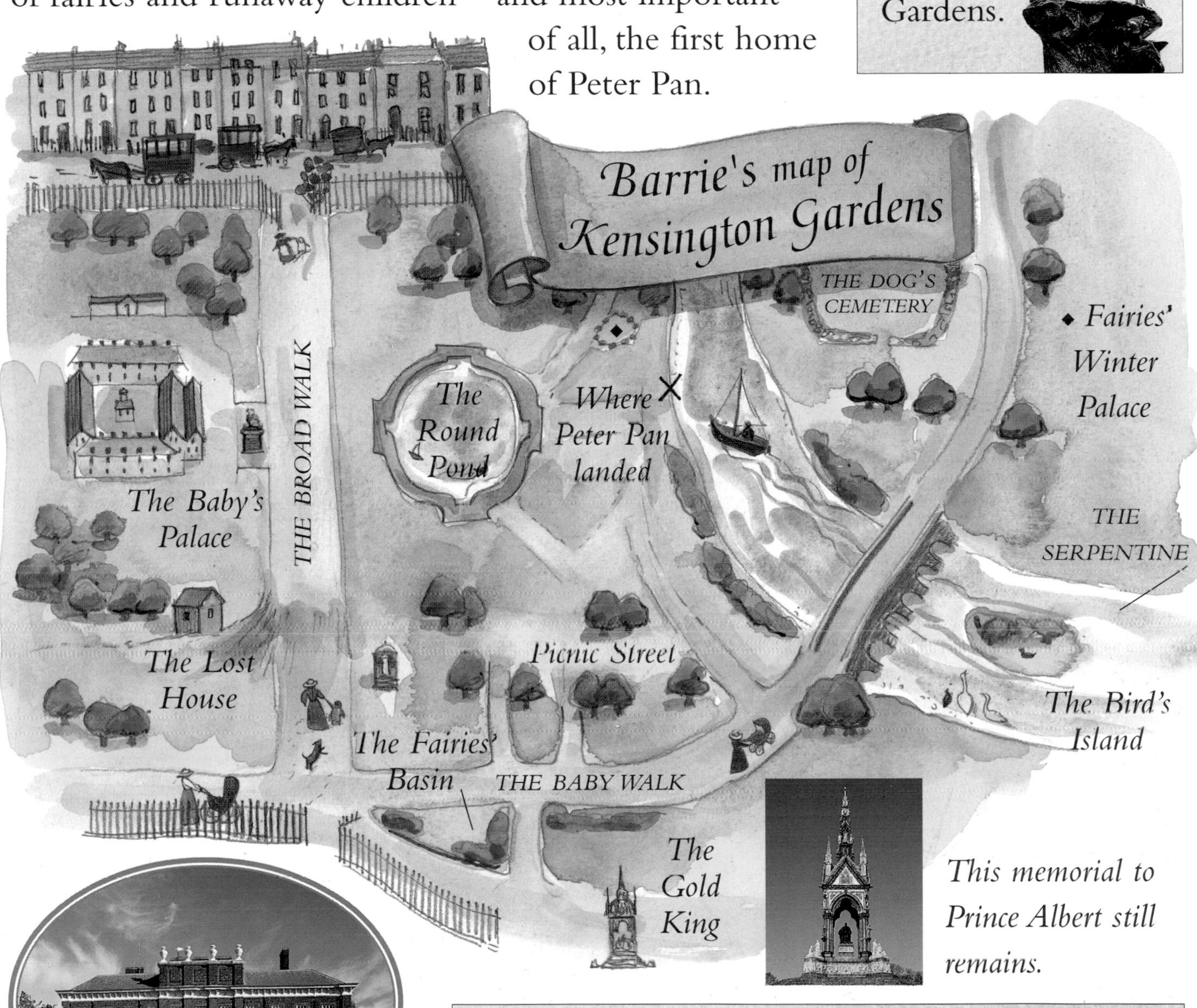

This memorial to Prince Albert still remains.

Barrie's "Baby's Palace" is Kensington Palace, which is owned by the British royal family. This was where Princess Diana lived.

✷ IN THE PARK

Kensington Gardens was a popular place for nannies to take the children to walk and play.

Peter Breaks Through

ALL CHILDREN, except one, grow up. Wendy knew she would grow up when she was two years old. She was playing in the garden and must have looked rather delightful, for Mrs. Darling put her hand on her heart and cried, "Oh, why can't you remain like this forever!" Wendy knew that two is the beginning of the end.

Mr. and Mrs. Darling lived in Bloomsbury, at No. 14, with Wendy, John, and Michael. You might have seen them going to Miss Fullerton's Kindergarten School, accompanied by their nurse. They were not rich, so this nurse was a prim Newfoundland dog called Nana.

There never was a simpler, happier family – until the coming of Peter Pan.

Mrs. Darling first heard of Peter when she was tidying up the children's minds after they were asleep, as is the nightly custom of every good mother. Occasionally she found things she could not understand, and the strangest of these was the word "Peter."

Mrs. Darling knew at once it was Peter Pan.

"Who is he, my pet?" she asked Wendy.

"He is Peter Pan, you know, Mother."

One morning some leaves had been found on the nursery floor.

"It is that Peter again!" said Wendy.

"Whatever do you mean, Wendy?" said Mrs. Darling.

Wendy explained she thought Peter sometimes came to the nursery in the night, sat at the foot of her bed, and played his pipes to her. She never woke up, so she didn't know how she knew, she just knew.

"I think he gets in through the window," she said.

"My love, it is three floors up," said Mrs. Darling, thinking Wendy had been dreaming. But the very next night, as Mrs. Darling was dozing by the nursery fire, the window blew open and a boy dropped onto the floor. He was accompanied by a strange light, which darted around the room. It was this light that woke Mrs. Darling. She awoke with a cry and somehow she knew at once that the boy was Peter Pan. He was a lovely boy, clothed in leaves and the juices that ooze out of trees. But the most entrancing thing was that he had all his baby teeth. When he saw Mrs. Darling was a grown-up, he gnashed his little pearls at her.

Mrs. Darling screamed. Nana entered, growled, and sprang at the boy who leaped through the window. When Mrs. Darling ran down to the street to look for his body, she could see nothing but what she thought was a shooting star.

Most wealthy families had a nurse to look after the children. To be like their neighbors the Darlings have a nurse, but they can only afford a dog!

Mrs. Darling returned to the nursery and found Nana with something in her mouth. Nana had closed the window too late to catch the boy, but had trapped his shadow. Mrs. Darling decided to roll up the shadow and put it in a drawer.

A week later, Mr. and Mrs. Darling were going to dine at No. 27. Mrs. Darling came in wearing her evening gown while Nana was trying to put the children to bed.

"I won't go," said Michael. "I won't."

Mr. Darling came rushing in with a crumpled tie in his hand.

"This tie, it will not tie," he yelled.

"Let me try, my dear," said Mrs. Darling, and she tied his tie for him. Mr. Darling forgot his rage and Mrs. Darling felt this was an opportunity to tell him about Peter. At first he pooh-poohed the story, but he became thoughtful when she showed him the shadow. They whispered about it until Nana came in with Michael's medicine.

"Won't!" Michael cried.

"Michael," said Mr. Darling. "When I was your age I took my medicine without a murmur. And I would take it now, if I hadn't lost the bottle."

Mrs. Darling decided to roll up the shadow.

"I know where it is, Father," Wendy cried, and was off before he could stop her.

"Michael first," Mr. Darling said.

"Father first," said Michael.

"Why not take it at the same time?" said Wendy. "One! Two! Three!"

Michael took his medicine. Mr. Darling slipped his behind his back. "Oh, Father!" Wendy exclaimed.

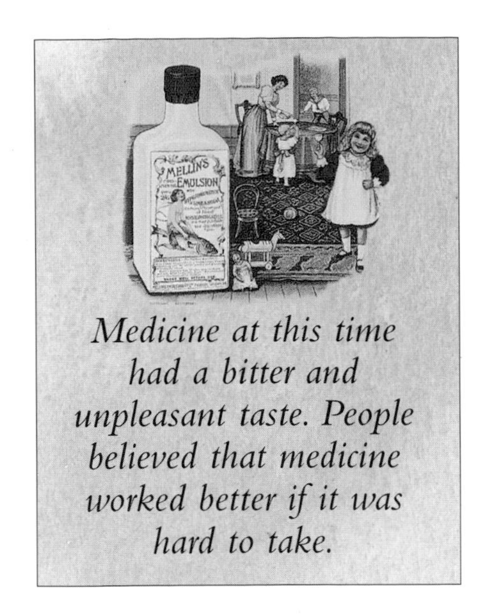

Medicine at this time had a bitter and unpleasant taste. People believed that medicine worked better if it was hard to take.

"Look here," he said, when Nana had gone into the bathroom. "I have just thought of a splendid joke. I will pour my medicine into Nana's bowl."

Nana returned, wagged her tail, and began lapping. Then she gave Mr. Darling an offended look and crept into her kennel.

"It was only a joke," Mr. Darling roared as Wendy hugged Nana. "Coddle her!" he shouted. "Nobody coddles me! I refuse to allow that dog in my nursery."

"George," Mrs. Darling whispered, "remember that boy."

Alas, he would not listen and dragged Nana from the nursery into the yard. Meanwhile, Mrs. Darling put the children to bed.

"Can anything harm us, Mother," yawned Michael, "after the night-lights are lit?"

"Nothing, precious," she said.

Later, the stars watched Mr. and Mrs. Darling making their way along the snow-covered street. As soon as the door of No. 27 closed behind them, the smallest star in the Milky Way screamed out, "Now, Peter!"

Mr. Darling dragged Nana from the nursery.

There was another light in the room now, looking for Peter's shadow. It was not really a light – it was a fairy no larger than your hand. A moment after the fairy's entrance, Peter dropped in.

"Tinker Bell," he called softly, "do you know where they put my shadow?"

The loveliest tinkle of golden laughter answered him. Peter jumped at the drawer where the tinkle came from and in a moment he had found his shadow. He had thought that he and his shadow would join like drops of water. When they did not, he was appalled. He tried to stick it on with soap but that also failed. At last, he sat on the floor and cried. His sobs woke Wendy.

"Boy," she said, "why are you crying? What is your name?"

Peter bowed graciously to her.

"Peter Pan, and I can't get my shadow to stick on."

"It must be sewn on," said Wendy, and she stitched the shadow onto Peter's foot. Peter jumped around in wild glee.

"How clever I am! Oh, the cleverness of me! But Wendy," he added quickly, "one girl is worth twenty boys."

Wendy uses a thimble to protect her finger when she sews on Peter's shadow. Most girls like Wendy learned to sew when they were very young.

"Well, that's sweet of you – I shall give you a kiss," Wendy declared.

Peter did not know what a kiss was, so he held out his hand. Wendy did not want to hurt his feelings and so she gave him her thimble instead.

"Now *I* shall give *you* a kiss," said Peter and dropped an acorn button into her hand. Wendy put his "kiss" on the chain around her neck.

"How old are you, Peter?" asked Wendy.

"I don't know," Peter replied. "I ran away the day I was born. I heard Father and Mother talking about what I was to be when I became a man, so I ran away to Kensington Gardens and lived among the fairies. Sometimes I still do. But mostly I live with the lost boys. They are children who fall out of their strollers when the nurse is looking the other way. But we have no female friends. Girls are too clever to fall out of strollers."

"I think it is lovely the way you talk about girls," said Wendy. "I will give you a kiss – I mean a thimble!" And she kissed him.

In return, Peter kissed her. Suddenly, Wendy screamed. It was Tink – she was pulling Wendy's hair.

Peter's sobs woke Wendy.

Peter knew there was not a moment to lose.

At this point Wendy's night-light blinked and gave such a yawn that the other two yawned also. Then all three went out.

"Wendy, fly with me to Neverland!" said Peter.

"I can't fly!"

"I'll teach you how to jump on the wind's back and then away we go."

"Can you teach John and Michael to fly too?"

"If you like."

"Wake up," Wendy cried. "Peter Pan has come to teach us to fly."

"I say, Peter," yawned John. "Can you really fly?"

Peter flew around the room. It looked easy and they tried it from their beds, but they always fell down.

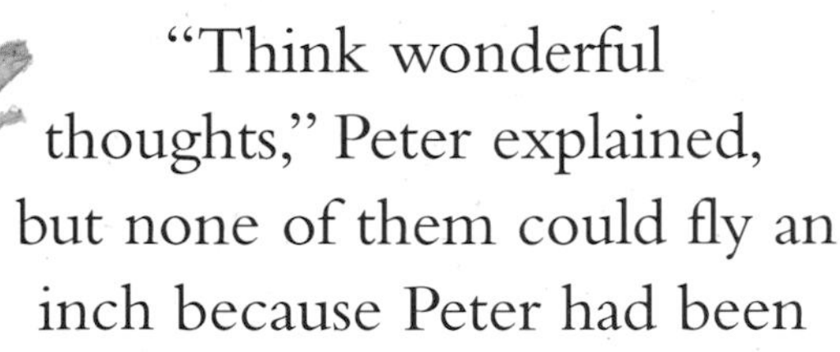

"Think wonderful thoughts," Peter explained, but none of them could fly an inch because Peter had been teasing them. People can't fly unless fairy dust has been blown on them. Fortunately it was all over one of Peter's hands and he blew some on each of them. "Wriggle your shoulders this way," he said, "and let's go."

Michael let go first.

"I flewed," he shouted.

John let go and met Wendy near the bathroom.

"Oh, lovely!"

"I say," cried John. "Why shouldn't we all go out!"

Wendy hesitated.

"There are mermaids," said Peter. "And pirates!"

"Pirates!" cried John, seizing his Sunday hat. "Let us go at once."

It was at this moment that Mr. and Mrs. Darling left No. 27. They looked up at the nursery window and saw three figures circling around in the air. No, not three but four! Peter knew there was not a moment to lose. "Come along!" he cried and soared out into the night, followed by John, Michael, Wendy – and Tinker Bell.

Mr. and Mrs. Darling rushed upstairs and into the nursery. But it was too late. The birds had flown.

At the time this story was written, most families did not have electricity. As daylight faded, oil lamps would be lit. Now that the children's oil lamps have gone out, the only light in the room is a magical one.

The Flight

"SECOND TO THE RIGHT and straight on till morning." That, Peter told Wendy, was the way to Neverland.

So great was the children's delight in flying that at first they wasted time circling around tall objects that caught their eye. Then they flew over the sea. Sometimes it was dark, and sometimes light, and now they were cold, and now too warm. When they were sleepy there was danger – for the moment they dropped off, down they fell.

Peter found this funny. "There he goes again," he would cry as Michael suddenly dropped like a stone.

"Save him!" cried Wendy, and Peter would dive through the air and catch Michael just before he hit the sea.

The children could fly strongly now, though they still kicked way too much. If they saw a cloud in front of them, the more they tried to avoid it, the more certainly did they bump into it. Peter showed them how to lie out flat on the wind. This was so pleasant that they tried it several times, and found they could even go to sleep safely.

And so they drew near Neverland. And, after many moons, Peter cried out, "There it is!"

Wendy and John and Michael stood on tiptoe in the air to get their first sight of the island.

"There's a lagoon," said Wendy.

"Wendy, look at the mermaids!" said John.

"I can see the smoke of the Indian camp," said Michael.

It was getting darker. They huddled close to Peter, flying so low that sometimes a tree grazed their faces. Peter sent Tink off to see what was ahead.

"There's a pirate ship beneath us," Peter said.

"Are there many pirates on the island?" asked John.

"Tons!"

"Who is captain of the pirates?"

"Hook!" answered Peter. "Captain James Hook. I cut off his right hand. He has an iron hook instead, and he claws with it. And you must promise me one thing."

John paled.

"If we meet Hook in open fight, you must leave him to me."

It was getting darker in the lagoon.

Tink was back again. She could not fly as slowly as the others, so she had to go around them in a circle.

"Tink tells me," Peter said, "that the pirates sighted us before the darkness came and they got Long Tom out."

"The big gun?" asked John.

"Yes," said Peter. "And if they see Tink's light, they will guess we are near and are sure to let fly."

"Tell Tink to go away at once," the three children cried at the same time, but Peter refused. "Then tell her to put her light out," begged Wendy.

"She can't put it out," said Peter. "It goes out by itself when she falls asleep."

"Then tell her to go to sleep at once," John said. "She can't sleep unless she's sleepy," Peter told him. "If only one of us had a pocket, we could carry her in it."

The sound of a pirate's cannon is deafeningly loud and warns Peter that the pirates are going to attack.

But they had set off in such a hurry, there was not a pocket among them. Suddenly, Peter had an idea – John's hat. Tink agreed to travel in it only if it was carried by hand. John took the hat at first, then Wendy took it, and this led to trouble – as we shall soon see. They flew on in silence, the stillest silence they had ever known.

"If only something would make a sound," Michael cried. As if in answer, the pirates fired Long Tom at them. The roar of it echoed through the mountains.

When at last the heavens were steady, John and Michael

found themselves alone in the darkness. Peter had been carried far out to sea while Wendy had been blown upward with no companion but Tinker Bell, who at once popped out of the hat. Tink was not bad, but she was jealous of Wendy. She flew back and forth, plainly meaning, "Follow me and all will be well." And Wendy, not knowing that Tink hated her, and staggering in her flight, followed the fairy to her doom.

The pirates fired Long Tom at them.

Down in Neverland, feeling that Peter was on his way back, the lost boys were out to greet their captain. There were six of them: Tootles, Nibs, Slightly, Curly, and the twins. Behind them were the pirates, and in their midst was Captain James Hook, a terrible man who treated his crew like dogs.

On the trail of the pirates came the Indians. They stole noiselessly down the warpath, led by Princess Tiger Lily. Last of all came a gigantic crocodile. All were going around and around the island, and did not meet because all were going at the same speed. The first to fall out of the moving circle were the boys. They flung themselves down on the grass close to their underground home.

Then the boys heard the pirates in the distance. Nibs ran off to see what was happening. The others darted down the hollow trees that led to their home underground.

As the pirates advanced, one of them, Smee, saw Nibs. Smee's pistol flashed out, but an iron claw gripped his shoulder.

"He is only one," said Hook. "I want all seven."

The pirates, except Hook and Smee, disappeared among the trees.

"I want Peter Pan," Hook said. "'Twas he who cut off my arm and flung it to a crocodile. That crocodile has followed me ever since."

Hook sat down on a large mushroom, "That crocodile would have had me before this, but by a lucky chance it swallowed a clock that goes *tick-tick* inside it. Before it can reach me I hear the tick and bolt."

Suddenly he jumped up. "I'm burning!" They examined the mushroom – it was a chimney. They had discovered the home underground! Hook started to plan how to capture the boys, until he heard a sound. *Tick-tick-tick-tick*.

"The crocodile!"

He bolted.

The Little House

ONE BY ONE the boys came out of hiding. Nibs appeared and pointed to the sky. "A great white bird is flying this way," he said.

It was Wendy. She was weary with flying and was moaning "Poor Wendy" to herself.

"There are birds called Wendies," said Slightly.

Then came the shrill voice of the jealous Tinker Bell calling out, "Peter wants you to shoot the Wendy."

Tootles had his bow and arrow ready.

"Quick, Tootles!" Tinker Bell shouted.

Tootles fired, and Wendy fluttered to the ground. The boys crowded around her.

Tootles had his bow and arrow ready.

"This is no bird," said Slightly. "It must be a lady."

"And we have killed her," Nibs said hoarsely.

They all whipped off their caps. At this tragic moment they heard Peter crow. This was his own special signal.

"Hide her," they whispered, and they gathered around Wendy just before Peter dropped in front of them.

"Greetings, boys," he cried. "I have brought a mother for you all at last. Have you seen her? She flew this way."

The lost boys always have their bows and arrows close at hand because they love to go hunting in Neverland.

They all stood back so that Peter could see Wendy lying there.

"Whose is this arrow?" Peter asked.

"Mine," said Tootles.

Just then, Wendy raised her arm.

"She lives!" cried Peter kneeling beside her. "The arrow hit this," he explained as he held up his acorn button that was on Wendy's necklace. "The kiss I gave her saved her life."

Suddenly, from overhead came a loud wail.

"That's Tink," said Curly, "she is crying because Wendy lives." They told Peter of Tink's crime.

"Listen, Tinker Bell," Peter cried. "I am your friend no more. Begone from me forever!"

She flew onto his shoulder and pleaded, but he brushed her off. Not until Wendy again raised her arm did Peter relent and say, "Well, not forever, but for a whole week."

Do you think Tinker Bell was grateful to Wendy for raising her arm? No! She wanted to pinch her. Fairies are strange indeed.

"Tinker Bell, begone from me forever," cried Peter.

They wondered what they should do with Wendy in her present state of health.

"Let us carry her down into the house," Curly suggested.

"No, you must not touch her," Peter said. "Let us build a house around her."

Just then, who should appear but John and Michael.

"Curly," said Peter, "make sure these boys help build the house."

"Build a house?" said John.

"For the Wendy," said Curly.

John was aghast. "But she is only a girl."

"That," explained Curly, "is why we are her servants."

The astounded brothers were dragged away to hack and carry.

"If only we knew what kind of house she likes best," said Nibs.

Immediately, without opening her eyes, Wendy began to sing:

"I wish I had a pretty house
The littlest ever seen,
With funny little red walls,
And roof of mossy green."

This house, built around Wendy, was the first "Wendy House." In Britain, a playhouse for children is now known as a "Wendy House."

They quickly built a little house.

"There is no knocker," said Peter, so Tootles gave him the sole of his shoe and this made an excellent knocker.

"There is no chimney," Peter said, so he snatched the hat off John's head, knocked out the top, and put it on the roof.

There was nothing left to do but to knock at the door.

"You should all look your best," Peter warned them, "first impressions are very important."

Peter knocked politely. The door opened, and Wendy came out.

"Where am I?" she said.

"Wendy lady," said Slightly, "for you we built this house."

"And we are your children," cried the twins.

They all went on their knees and cried, "Wendy lady, be our mother."

"Should I?" Wendy said. "Very well. I will do my best. Come inside, you naughty children. I am sure your feet are damp."

By and by Wendy tucked the boys in bed in their home underground, while she slept in the little house. Peter kept watch outside, his sword drawn, for the pirates were lurking and wolves were prowling. After a time he fell asleep and some fairies had to climb over him on their way home from a party.

The boys were in bed in their home underground.

The cooking kept Wendy's nose to the pot.

The Lagoon

WENDY DID NOT HAVE a moment to waste because those boys gave her so much to do. The cooking kept her nose to the pot, and when she sewed and darned their clothes she would fling up her arms and exclaim, "I sometimes think that children are more trouble than they are worth!"

A mermaid is a wonderful creature with a woman's upper body and a fish's tail. In this story the mermaids live in the calm waters of the lagoon.

There were adventures in Neverland every day, especially in the lagoon. The blue lagoon was at the edge of the island, and the children often spent long summer days swimming or floating and playing mermaid games in the water. The mermaids never let themselves be caught, but they sat combing their hair and splashing the children if they came too close. Wendy was often at the lagoon, especially on sunny days after the rain, when the mermaids come up in extraordinary numbers to play with their bubbles.

One afternoon the children were all sitting on Marooners' Rock. (It was called this because the rock is submerged when the tide rises, and so evil captains put sailors there to drown.) The boys were dozing, and Wendy was busy sewing when a change came over the lagoon.

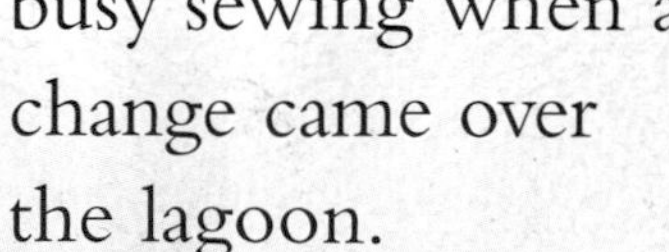

The sun went away, and shadows stole across the water. Suddenly Wendy heard the sound of muffled oars.

Peter sprang up, and with one warning cry he roused the others. "Pirates!" he cried, and a strange smile played about his face. "Dive!" There was a gleam of legs, and instantly the lagoon seemed deserted.

The boat drew nearer. It was the pirate dinghy. Three figures were in it – Smee, another pirate called Starkey, and Tiger Lily, the Indian princess. Her hands and ankles were tied and she knew she was to be left on the rock to perish. Yet her face was motionless – she was the daughter of a chief and must die as the daughter of a chief.

The sun went away, and shadows stole across the water.

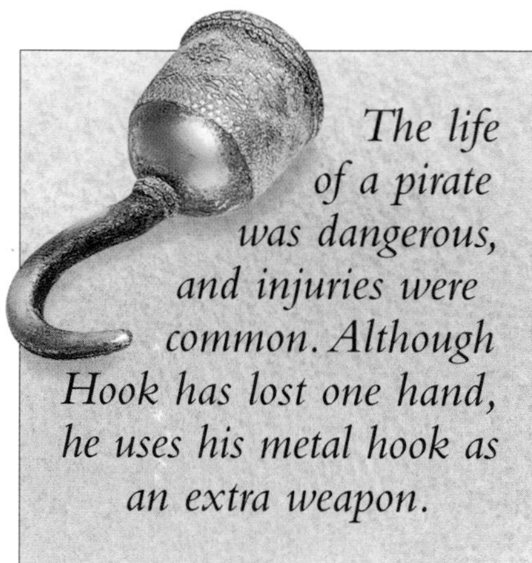

The life of a pirate was dangerous, and injuries were common. Although Hook has lost one hand, he uses his metal hook as an extra weapon.

Quite near the rock, but out of sight, two heads were bobbing – Peter's and Wendy's.

"Ahoy there, you lubbers," Peter called, in a marvelous imitation of Hook's voice.

"It's the captain," said the pirates. "He must be swimming out to us."

"We are putting Tiger Lily on the rock," called Smee.

"Set her free," came the astonishing answer.

"But, Captain –"

"At once, d'ye hear," cried Peter, "or I'll plunge my hook into you."

"Better do as the captain orders," said Starkey, and he cut Tiger Lily's cord. She slid into the water.

"Boat ahoy!" Hook's voice rang over the lagoon, and this time it was not Peter who had spoken. The real Hook was in the water, and he was swimming to the boat.

Peter saw he was higher up the rock than his foe.

He pulled himself into it and said in a melancholy voice, "Those boys have found a mother."

"Could we not kidnap her and make her *our* mother?" asked Smee.

"A princely scheme!" cried Hook. "We shall seize the children, make the boys walk the plank, and Wendy shall be our mother."

Suddenly he remembered Tiger Lily.

"Where is the prisoner?" he demanded.

"We let her go," Smee answered. "On your orders."

"I gave no such order," said Hook. When Smee told him about the strange voice, Hook became worried.

"Spirit of the lagoon," Hook called out, "can you hear me?"

"Odds, bobs, hammer and tongs, I hear you," answered Peter in Hook's voice.

"Who are you, stranger?" Hook demanded. "Are you a boy?"

"I am Peter Pan! Are you ready, boys?"

"Aye, aye," came from various parts of the lagoon.

"Then thrash those pirates!"

The fight was short and sharp. A flash of steel here, followed by a cry or a whoop there. Hook wriggled overboard. He rose to the rock as Peter climbed it on the opposite side. Suddenly they were face to face. Peter gnashed his teeth with joy. He snatched a knife from Hook's belt and was about to strike when Peter saw he was higher up the rock than his foe. It was not a fair fight. He gave the pirate a hand to help him up. It was then that Hook bit him.

The crocodile slithered onto the rock.

It was not the pain but the unfairness of the bite that dazed Peter.

Twice Hook's iron hand clawed him, but just when it seemed all was lost, Hook dived into the water. He struck wildly for the ship, his face white with fear, for the crocodile had slithered onto the rock in dogged pursuit. The boys would have cheered, but they were uneasy because they could not see Peter and Wendy. They found the dinghy and began to row home, calling out, "Peter! Wendy!"

A cold silence fell over the lagoon, then a feeble cry, "Help! Help!"

Two small figures lay on the rock, the water rising.

"We must go," Wendy said.

"Yes," Peter answered faintly.

"Shall we swim or fly, Peter?"

"I can't do either, Wendy, Hook has wounded me."

As he spoke, something brushed against him. It was the tail of a kite Michael had made some days before.

"The kite could carry you!" said Peter.

Wendy said she wouldn't go without him. But Peter insisted. He tied the tail around her and with a "Good-bye, Wendy," he pushed her off the rock. Soon she was out of sight. Peter was left alone on the lagoon, afraid at last. Next moment, he was smiling. A drum was beating within him saying, "To die will be an awfully big adventure."

Peter knows what a sacrifice the Never Bird has made by giving him her nest of eggs – a bird's most precious possession.

The waters were nibbling at his feet when he noticed an odd thing – the Never Bird making desperate efforts to reach him on her nest. She wanted to give the nest to him, even though there were eggs in it. With a mighty effort she pushed the nest against the rock, then up she flew.

Peter clutched the nest and waved his thanks to the bird. Inside, there were two large white eggs. Peter lifted them up and suddenly he had an idea. On the rock there was a wooden stave and on the stave the pirate Starkey had hung his hat, watertight and with a broad brim. Peter put the eggs in the hat and set the hat on the lagoon. It floated beautifully.

Peter pulled the stave from the rock, placed it on the nest as a mast and hung his shirt on it as a sail. Then he skimmed across the lagoon.

Peter skimmed across the lagoon.

The Never Bird fluttered down and sat snugly on her eggs. The hat was such a great success that all Never Birds now build that shape of nest with a broad brim.

Great was the rejoicing when Peter reached the home underground. Every boy had adventures to tell, but perhaps the biggest adventure of all was that they were several hours late for bed.

Peter was left alone on the lagoon, afraid at last.

The Home Underground

EVER SINCE Peter had rescued Tiger Lily from the pirates, the Indians had become friends with the children, and at night they guarded their home underground against pirate attacks.

One evening, the Indians were sitting above the lost boys' home, keeping watch. Inside, the children were having their evening meal, which happened to be make-believe tea, and what with all their chattering and shouting, the noise was deafening. When tea was over, the children sang and danced until at last they all got into bed for Wendy's story.

Peter sat next to Wendy, looking uncomfortable.

"What is wrong, Peter?" Wendy asked.

"It is only pretend, isn't it, that I am their father?"

"Oh, yes," said Wendy a little sadly.

"You see," he continued, "it would make me seem so old to be their real father."

Wendy nodded. Then she began her story.

"There was once a gentleman and a lady called Mr. and Mrs. Darling," Wendy began. "They had three children and a nanny called Nana. But Mr. Darling was angry with Nana and chained her up in the yard, so all the children flew away."

The Indians were sitting above the home underground.

"That's a very sad story," said the first twin.

"No," said Wendy. "The mother always left the window open for her children, so they stayed away for years and had a lovely time."

"I thought my mother would keep the window open for me, so I stayed away for moons," snapped Peter. "But when I flew back, the window was closed and there was another little boy sleeping in my bed."

"Wendy, let us go home!" cried John and Michael.

"Yes," Wendy said, clutching them. "Peter, will you make the necessary arrangements?"

"If you wish it," said Peter coolly, as if he did not mind at all, which of course he did.

The children were having their evening meal.

Panic-stricken at the thought of losing Wendy, the lost boys advanced upon her threateningly.

"We won't let her go," cried Tootles.

"Chain her up," said Nibs.

But Peter would keep no girl against her will.

"I will ask the Indians to guide you through the woods. Then Tinker Bell will take you across the sea," he said.

"Dear boys," sighed Wendy, "if you come with me I feel sure I can get my father and mother to adopt you."

"Can we go, Peter?" they all cried imploringly.

Peter nodded and immediately they rushed to get their things.

Peter stayed where he was.

"Get your things, Peter," Wendy cried.

"No," he said, pretending not to care, "I am not going with you."

"Yes you must, Peter," cried Wendy.

"No!" said Peter. "No fuss, no blubbering. Good-bye, Wendy."

"You will take your medicine?" said Wendy anxiously.

Peter nodded. "Ready, Tinker Bell?"

Tink disappeared, but no one else moved, because it was at this moment that the pirates made their dreadful attack upon the Indians.

The pirate attack was a complete surprise, and the fighting ended almost as soon as it began. Many Indians perished. Only Tiger Lily and a few other warriors managed to fight their way out.

Underground, Peter waited to hear the outcome of the battle.

"If the Indians have won," Peter said, "they will beat their tom-tom drum."

But Hook, listening carefully at the mouths of the trees, overheard Peter's words. He signaled to the pirate Smee, who was sitting on the tom-tom drum, to beat it loudly. Twice Smee beat upon the drum, and then stopped to listen gleefully.

"It must be an Indian victory!" cried Peter.

The lost boys were taken by the pirates.

Confident of their safety, the lost boys said good-bye to Peter and emerged from their trees. Immediately they were taken by the pirates and thrown at Hook's feet.

But Wendy received different treatment. Hook offered her his arm and escorted her to the spot where the lost boys were being gagged.

The children were flung into Wendy's little house, and the pirates raised it on their shoulders and set off through the woods. But Hook stayed behind.

Hook held his breath and crept toward a tree. All was silent as he stepped into the hollow tree trunk and dropped down to the home underground. There lay Peter, unaware of the tragic events above-ground, fast asleep on his bed. Silently, Hook took a step forward. He caught sight of Peter's medicine and quickly dribbled five drops of a deadly poison into it. Then he wormed his way up the tree again and, muttering to himself, stole away through the woods.

Peter slept on until he was wakened by a soft, cautious tapping on the door of his tree. It was Tink.

"Oh, you could never guess," she cried, and told him of the capture of Wendy and the boys.

"I'll rescue Wendy," he cried, leaping up. As he leaped he thought of something he could do to please Wendy. He could take his medicine. Peter reached for it.

Hook dribbled five drops of a deadly poison into Peter's medicine.

Tink drained the medicine to the dregs.

"No!" shrieked Tinker Bell, and as Peter raised the cup she flew between his lips and the medicine and drained it to the dregs.

"Why, Tink, how dare you drink my medicine?" Peter said crossly.

But she did not answer. Already she was reeling in the air.

"What is the matter with you?" cried Peter, suddenly afraid.

"It was poisoned, Peter," she told him softly. "And now I am going to be dead."

But then in a voice so faint that Peter could just make out her words, she told Peter she could get well again if children believed in fairies.

Peter flung out his arms. There were no children there, and it was nighttime, but Peter addressed all those children who might be asleep dreaming of Neverland.

"Do you believe?" he cried out. "If you believe, clap your hands – don't let Tink die."

Many clapped. Some didn't. A few little beasts hissed, but already Tink was saved. She was soon dashing around the room faster than ever.

"And now to rescue Wendy," cried Peter.

He was terribly happy.

Peter knows that if you believe in something you can make it real. By believing in fairies, children keep Tink alive.

The Pirate Ship

OVER AT KIDD'S CREEK, on the *Jolly Roger*, a few of the pirates leaned over the side of the ship, others sprawled by barrels over games of dice and cards, and the rest were dancing noisily.

"Quiet!" Hook cried. At once the din was hushed. "Are all the children chained so they cannot fly away?"

"Aye, aye."

"Then hoist the boys up."

The wretched prisoners were dragged from the hold, all except Wendy.

"Now then," Hook said, "six of you walk the plank tonight, but I have room for two cabin boys. Which of you is it to be?"

"I don't think my mother would like me to be a pirate," said Tootles. "Would your mother like you to be a pirate, Slightly?"

"I don't think so," said Slightly. "Would your mother like you to be a pirate, twin?"

"Did you never want to be a pirate?"

"Stow this gab," roared Hook. "You, boy, did you never want to be a pirate?" he said to John.

"I once thought of calling myself Red-handed Jack," John admitted.

"We'll call you that here if you join."

"What would you call me if I join?" Michael demanded.

"Blackbeard Joe."

"Will we still be respectful subjects of the King?" John inquired.

"You'll swear, 'Down with the King.'"

Captain Hook's ship is called the Jolly Roger, *which is also the name for the pirate flag. The symbol of the skull was used to frighten other ships into immediate surrender.*

Smee tied Wendy to the mast.

"Then I refuse," cried John.

"That seals your doom," Hook roared. "Bring up their mother. Get the plank ready."

Wendy was brought to him.

"Silence, for a mother's last words to her children," he said.

Wendy was brave.

"These are my last words, dear boys," she said. "I feel that I have a message to you from your real mothers, and it is this: 'We hope our sons will die like English gentlemen.'"

"Tie her up," said Hook.

Smee tied her to the mast. There was an eerie silence. Hook took a step toward Wendy. But he never reached her, because he heard a noise. It was the terrible *tick-tick* of the crocodile.

"Hide me," Hook cried. The pirates gathered around him and turned away from the thing that was coming on board.

But it was Peter, not the crocodile, who was making the ticking sound! Peter signed to the children not to burst into applause and then vanished into the cabin.

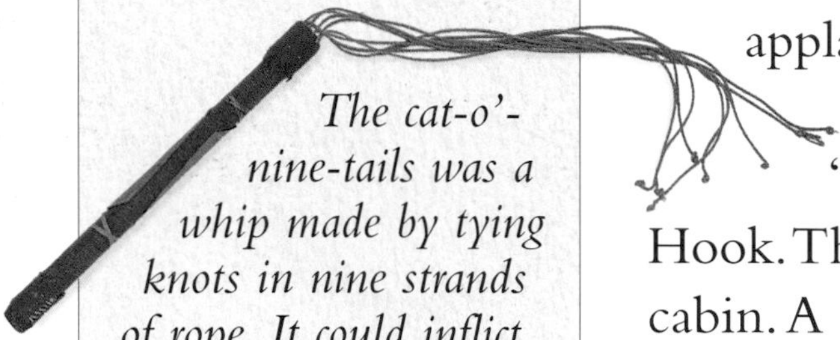

The cat-o'-nine-tails was a whip made by tying knots in nine strands of rope. It could inflict terrible wounds.

"It's gone, captain," Smee said, looking up.

"Fetch the cat-o'-nine-tails, Jukes," said Hook. The pirate Jukes strode confidently into the cabin. A dreadful screech wailed through the ship. Then a crowing sound. Another of the pirates ran into the cabin, but he tottered out moments later.

"Jukes is dead," he said in a hollow voice. "There's something in there. The thing you heard crowing *doodle-doo*."

"Go and fetch me that doodle-doo," commanded Hook.

The pirate went once more into the cabin, and again they all heard a screech and then a crow. Hook turned to the children.

"You can fight the doodle-doo!" he cried.

The boys were pushed into the cabin. Peter quickly freed them, and together they crept outside. They could see Hook and his pirates waiting on deck, too scared to look at the cabin door. Peter reached Wendy and cut her free. Then he cried, "Down, boys, and at 'em!"

In a moment the clash of arms resounded through the ship. The pirates ran hither and thither. Some jumped into the sea, others fell by the sword. Soon only Hook remained.

Hook fell into the jaws of the crocodile.

"Put up your swords, boys, this man is mine," cried Peter. He lunged fiercely, piercing Hook in the ribs. The sword fell from Hook's hand.

"Peter Pan, who and what are you?" Hook cried.

"I am youth, I am joy!" Peter answered.

Hook ran to the weapon house and lit a fuse. "In two minutes," he cried, "the ship will be blown to pieces!"

Peter darted into the room, came out with the bomb, and calmly flung it overboard. Hook got ready to throw himself into the sea, unaware that the crocodile, whose clock had finally stopped, was waiting. Hook had one last triumph. He invited Peter to push him overboard, so Peter prodded him with his foot. "Bad form," jeered Hook as he fell into the jaws of the crocodile.

Some pirates fell into the sea.

The Return Home

FAR FROM NEVERLAND, back in the home from which the three children had taken flight so long ago, Mr. and Mrs. Darling were trying to continue their lives. The only change that could be seen in the night-nursery was that between nine and six the kennel was not there. Mr. Darling felt in his bones that all the blame was his for having chained Nana up, and he had decided to live in the kennel.

"This is the place for me," he said sadly as he crawled into it.

Every morning the kennel was carried with Mr. Darling in it to a taxi, which took him to his office, and he returned home in the same way at six.

Mr. Darling had decided to live in the kennel.

It was a Thursday evening. Mr. Darling was in his kennel feeling drowsy.

"Will you play me to sleep on the nursery piano?" he asked Mrs. Darling, and as she crossed to the day-nursery he added, "And shut the window."

"Never ask me to do that," she cried. "The window must always be left open for them, always."

Mrs. Darling went to the nursery and played the piano. Soon Mr. Darling was asleep, and did not stir when Peter Pan and Tinker Bell flew in.

"Quick, Tink," Peter whispered, "close the window. Now when Wendy comes she will think her mother has barred her out and she will have to come back to me."

Nannies usually slept in the nursery to keep an eye on the children. Since Nana is a dog, she has a kennel, not a bed!

He peeped into the day-nursery to see who was playing. It was Wendy's mother.

"She is a pretty lady. Her mouth is full of thimbles." Peter said.

He did not know the tune she was playing, but he knew it was saying, "Come back, Wendy, Wendy, Wendy . . . "

"You will never see Wendy again, lady," Peter cried, turning away, "for the window is barred."

The music stopped and when Peter peeped in to see why, he saw Mrs. Darling had two tears in her eyes.

"She wants me to unbar the window," thought Peter. "But I won't."

Peter could see that Mrs. Darling's tears were still there.

"She's very fond of Wendy," he said. "But we can't both have her."

But Mrs. Darling could not stop her tears.

"Oh, all right," Peter cried. Then he unbarred the window. "Come on, Tink," he cried, "we don't want silly mothers." And he flew away.

Peter peeped into the day-nursery.

And so Wendy, John, and Michael found the window open for them. But the youngest one, Michael, had already forgotten his home.

"John," he said, "I think I have been here before."

"Of course you have, silly. There is your old bed."

"So it is," said Michael, without much conviction.

"Look!" cried John. "The kennel! There's a man inside it."

"It's Father," exclaimed Wendy.

"He is not as big as the pirates I saw," John said.

It was then that Mrs. Darling began playing again.

"It's Mother," cried Wendy. "Let us all slip into our beds and be there when she comes in, just as if we had never been away."

And so when Mrs. Darling went back to the night-nursery she could hardly believe her eyes. All the beds were occupied! She stretched out her arms, and Wendy, John, and Michael slipped out of bed and ran to her.

Wendy, John, and Michael ran to Mrs. Darling.

Mr. and Mrs. Darling agreed to adopt the lost boys waiting outside. As for Peter he brushed against the window and called out, "Wendy, come with me to your little house."

When Mrs. Darling saw Peter, she made this offer – Wendy could go with him for a week every year to do his spring cleaning.

Peter came for Wendy at the end of the first year, forgot to come for her the one after that, but came the next – and that was the last time the girl Wendy ever saw him. Years passed and Peter did not return. Wendy married and had a daughter called Jane.

One night when Jane was asleep in her bed, and Wendy was sitting on the nursery floor, the window blew open and Peter appeared.

"Wendy," he said. "It's spring-cleaning time."

"I cannot come, Peter," she said. "I've forgotten how to fly. I grew up a long time ago," and she ran out of the room to hide her sadness.

"But you promised not to," cried Peter, and he sat down on the floor and sobbed. His sobs woke Jane.

"Why are you crying?" Jane asked.

Peter rose and bowed to her. When Wendy returned she found Peter sitting on the bedpost, while Jane was flying round the room.

So Peter took Jane instead of Wendy to Neverland to do the spring cleaning. And because Peter never grew up, when Jane had her own children, they flew away with Peter too, and so it will always be, as long as there are children!

Peter never grew up.

The Legendary Boy

EVERYONE HAS HEARD of Peter Pan. He is the baby boy who ran away from his parents to live in Kensington Gardens. He is the leader in Neverland. But most of all, Peter Pan is the little part of all of us – the part that does not want to grow up.

The name 'Pan' comes from the Greek nature god Pan, who loved music and played on pipes.

✷ THE MAKING OF PETER PAN

Peter Pan first appeared in 1902 in a book written by J. M. Barrie called *The Little White Bird*. In 1904 Barrie produced a stage play called *Peter Pan*. It was a huge success. The legend of Peter Pan had begun.

In 1906 Barrie wrote another book called *Peter Pan in Kensington Gardens*, in which he told about more adventures of Peter Pan.

✷ THE FAIRY TINKER

Peter Pan explains to Wendy that the fairy is called "Tinker Bell" because she mends pots and kettles, like a tinker.

✷ THE LOST BOYS

The lost boys are babies who fall out of their strollers when their nannies are not looking.

✷ BE MY FWENDY
The name Wendy comes from one of the children that Barrie knew, Margaret Henley. She could not say the word "friend" – she said "fwendy" instead. And so the name Wendy was born.

Barrie's favourite book was Treasure Island, *by R. L. Stevenson – a book filled with pirates. Barrie was inspired by this book to create his own villainous pirate, Captain Hook.*

Since Peter Pan flew onto the stage, the play has been produced hundreds of times. Now you can read the story in a number of languages, and see it on stage and in movies all over the world.

An early version, illustrated by Arthur Rackham.

Peter Pan in Japanese

Disney's version of Peter Pan *has been a huge success.*

© Disney

Ian McKellen as Captain Hook in a 1997–8 production of Peter Pan.

The pirates' ship, the Jolly Roger

✷ NEVERLAND
Where there is Peter Pan there is Neverland, or Never Never Land, as Barrie sometimes called it. This imaginary world full of pirates, Indians, mermaids, and fairies is just what you want it to be – the perfect dream world of adventures.

Barrie's Story

Barrie's signature

J. M. Barrie (1860–1937)

J. M. BARRIE WAS BORN in a small Scottish town called Kirriemuir in 1860. The origins of *Peter Pan* start early in Barrie's childhood. His older brother, David, was killed in a skating accident at the age of thirteen. Barrie realized that while he was getting older, David would always be thirteen – he was the boy who would never grow up.

Barrie's home near Kensington Gardens

✷ BARRIE THE WRITER

Barrie moved to London and became a successful writer. He married, and although he had no children of his own, he started to write stories for children. While walking in Kensington Gardens, he met the five Llewelyn Davies children, who together inspired Barrie to develop the story and character of Peter Pan.

Michael Llewelyn Davies dressed up as Peter Pan.

✷ CHILDREN'S HOSPITAL

In 1929 Barrie gave all the rights to *Peter Pan* to the Great Ormond Street Children's Hospital in London. Peter Pan soon became a symbol of hope for children everywhere.

THE HOSPITAL FOR SICK CHILDREN
GREAT ORMOND STREET, LONDON, W.C.1.

Peter Pan League

This is to Certify that

has been enrolled as a member of the PETER PAN LEAGUE.

Signed

Peter Pan

Membership No. Date

A Peter Pan League certificate from Great Ormond Street Hospital.